Two forest friends have picked some
fresh raspberries for a new forest baby.
Scratch and sniff for a sweet smell
of the baby's first raspberries.

Walt Disney Productions BAMBI'S Fragrant Forest

Based on the original story by Felix Salten

 Golden Press • New York

Western Publishing Company, Inc.
Racine, Wisconsin

Fourth Printing, 1976

Bambi was born in a thicket in the deep woods.
It was a shady place of ferns and pines and soft moss.

The new little deer sniffed.
The thicket smelled good, a mixture of the trees and the earth.

Scratch and sniff here to find out how Bambi's thicket home smelled. Have you ever been in a forest? Did it smell like this?

From all over the forest many animal families came to welcome Bambi.

Bambi tried to stand up, but his legs were not strong enough yet.

Up he got, but down he fell—oops—right into a strawberry patch.

Scratch and sniff these delicious strawberries. Don't you wish you could have some to eat?

"He's very wobbly!" giggled Thumper.
"Hush now," said Thumper's mother.

Thumper showed Bambi the forest.
Bambi saw something beautiful fly by.
"That's a butterfly," said Thumper.

Bambi saw more beautiful things.
"Butterfly!" he said.
"No, those are flowers," laughed Thumper,
"and they are called roses."

The rose has one of the
loveliest fragrances of all
the flowers. Scratch and
sniff here so you can smell
the beautiful roses.

A skunk sat up in the rosebed.
"Flower?" asked Bambi.
Thumper just rolled all over the place laughing.

"No, Bambi," he said. "Not *flower*—skunk."
"Flower," said Bambi again.
And so, Flower it was.

Here is a cedar from
Bambi's forest. Scratch and
sniff. Have you ever smelled
a cedar tree before?

Everywhere that Bambi went, his nose was busy sniffing.
He smelled the tall cedar trees.

His ears were also busy listening.
He heard a brook bubble;
he heard the birds and the wind sing in the trees.

Everywhere that Bambi went his eyes were busy looking.
He saw the tiniest toadstools, the tallest trees,
the high, blue sky, and many, many, animal friends.
How many animals can you name?

But everywhere that Bambi went his
legs were still busy wobbling.
Down again he tumbled, right into a
delicious patch of mint.
His nose twitched happily
as he sniffed.

Scratch and sniff this patch
of mint. Doesn't it smell
good? Mint leaves are used
in some kinds of candy.
Have you ever tasted any?

"Mother," said Bambi, "what else can I discover?"
"Bambi, there's so much," his mother said.
"Come, now I will show you the meadow."

First they came to a stream.

Fish swam swiftly under the water.

A frog plopped in. Waterskaters and
whirligig beetles skimmed across the top.

Bambi's mother leaped across the stream.

Bambi did too! He was learning quickly. This time he didn't fall down.

Bambi followed his mother farther through the forest.
The sky grew dark.
A sudden rainstorm made everything wet and shiny.

And it made the woods smell wonderful.
Bambi followed his nose to some wild sage plants.

Scratch and sniff the
fragrant sage. Do you have
any wild sage growing in
your yard?

At last they stood by the meadow.
It was a bright golden place.
No trees or vines or moss grew there.
Only grasses, tall, sweet-smelling
grasses.
The big sky was higher and wider
than Bambi had ever imagined it
could be.

And there was so much space for running!
Bambi ran and ran and galloped and leaped high over the waving grasses. He was so excited by the world around him.

Scratch and sniff to smell the grass in Bambi's meadow. It's the smell of the wide outdoors.